RALPH
and the Rocket Ship

by Alyssa Satin Capucilli ★ illustrated by Henry Cole

Ready-to-Read

Simon Spotlight

New York   London   Toronto   Sydney   New Delhi

For Stella Hazel and Dylan Lazarus,
my newest stars!
—A. S. C.

For H. R. G.
—H. C.

SIMON SPOTLIGHT
An imprint of Simon & Schuster Children's Publishing Division
1230 Avenue of the Americas, New York, New York 10020
This Simon Spotlight edition September 2016
Text copyright © 2016 by Alyssa Satin Capucilli
Illustrations copyright © 2016 by Henry Cole
All rights reserved, including the right of reproduction in whole or in part in any form.
SIMON SPOTLIGHT, READY-TO-READ, and colophon are registered trademarks of Simon & Schuster, Inc.
For information about special discounts for bulk purchases, please contact Simon & Schuster Special Sales at
1-866-506-1949 or business@simonandschuster.com.
Manufactured in the United States of America 0217 LAK
10 9 8 7 6 5 4 3 2
This book has been cataloged with the Library of Congress.
ISBN 978-1-4814-5866-5 (pbk)
ISBN 978-1-4814-5867-2 (hc)
ISBN 978-1-4814-5868-9 (eBook)

This is Ralph.

Ralph loves things that go fast!

Ralph loves cars.

He loves trains and trucks.

Most of all,

he loves rocket ships.

One day, Ralph asked
for a rocket ship.

"A rocket ship can take me
up to the stars,"
said Ralph.

"A rocket ship can take me
to the moon!" he said.

"A rocket ship can take me
to planets far, far away!
Zip! Zoom! Whoosh!"

"A rocket ship is too big,"
said Ralph's mother.
"Here is your train."

"Choo! Choo! Chug!"
Ralph's train could not
reach the stars.

"A rocket ship is too tall," said his father.

"Here is your tractor."

"Clink! Clank! Clunk!"
Ralph's tractor could not
fly to the moon.

"There must be some way
to get a rocket ship,"
said Ralph.

"Zip! Zoom! Whoosh!
But how?"

Ralph thought and thought.

He thought some more.

And then . . .

Stack!

Stack!

Tap!

Tap!

Bang! Bang!

Tape, tape, tape, tape!

"10-9-8-7-6-5-4-3-2-1 . . .

Blast off!" shouted Ralph.

Ralph's rocket ship went up
to the stars, and the moon,
and the faraway planets.

Ralph's rocket ship took
him wherever he wanted
to go.

"Zip! Zoom! Whoosh!"

And there was
plenty of room
for his friend Katy too.